鍾雲如 著
Poems by Chung Yun-ru

孔維仁 譯
Translated by Consonni Paolo

# 南 方 之 星

## The South Star

鍾雲如漢英雙語詩集
Chinese – English

台灣詩叢 • Taiwan Poetry Series 03

# 【總序】詩推台灣意象

叢書策劃／李魁賢

進入21世紀，台灣詩人更積極走向國際，個人竭盡所能，在詩人朋友熱烈參與支持下，策劃出席過印度、蒙古、古巴、智利、緬甸、孟加拉、馬其頓等國舉辦的國際詩歌節，並編輯《台灣心聲》等多種詩選在各國發行，使台灣詩人心聲透過作品傳佈國際間。接續而來的國際詩歌節邀請愈來愈多，已經有應接不暇的趨向。

多年來進行國際詩交流活動最困擾的問題，莫如臨時編輯帶往國外交流的選集，大都應急處理，不但時間緊迫，且選用作品難免會有不週。因此，興起策劃【台灣詩叢】雙語詩系的念頭。若台灣詩人平常就有雙語詩集出版，隨時可以應用，詩作交流與詩人交誼雙管齊下，更具實際成效，對台灣詩的國際交流活動，當更加順利。

以【台灣】為名，著眼點當然有鑑於台灣文學在國際間名目不彰，台灣詩人能夠有機會在國際努力開拓空間，非為個人建立知名度，而是為推展台灣意象的整體事功，期待開創台灣文學的長久景象，才能奠定寶貴的歷史意義，台灣文學終必在世界文壇上佔有地位。

實際經驗也明顯印證，台灣詩人參與國際詩交流活動，很受重視，帶出去的詩選集也深受歡迎，從近年外國詩人和出版社與本人合作編譯台灣詩選，甚至主動翻譯本人詩集在各國文學雜誌或詩刊發表，進而出版外譯詩集的情況，大為增多，即可充分證明。

　　承蒙秀威資訊科技公司一本支援詩集出版初衷，慨然接受【台灣詩叢】列入編輯計畫，對台灣詩的國際交流，提供推進力量，希望能有更多各種不同外語的雙語詩集出版，形成進軍國際的集結基地。

2017.02.15誌

# 目次

# 強大的力量

強大的力量
隱藏在最弱小的生命裡
小小的
在生命起跑點上微弱的氣息
他們總能夠喚起我昏昏欲睡的心靈
悄悄說

愛　不能等

# 塵囂之上

塵囂之下
萬古長空
分秒必爭

爭著種瓜
讚美種瓜的人
爭著種豆
讚美種豆的人

除了讚美
還有什麼更悅耳的曲調呢

# 傾聽

〈我要輕輕聽，我要輕輕聽……。〉

5 4 3 2 1

1 2 3 4 5

那是風的傳遞

我如何分辨其中的真理

這世界有許多美妙的聲音

在我們周圍充滿著

偶而也有尖銳聲響

讓我們想掩起耳朵逃避

這一切關於

5 4 3 2 1

1 2 3 4 5

意涵著每一個人　每一件事　每一個聲音

多麼活潑的存在著

而我們也用感覺去在意著

我們無法改變而感覺失落
唯有尋找主的聲音
引領在所有的聲音之上
啊　多麼悅耳
多麼平安

# 追尋

生命如迷宮彎彎曲曲
踏出步履
卻使我們常常疑惑
並豎起遲鈍的耳朵
在迷宮中來來回回

追尋真理
一步一步　不疾不徐
即使踏遍
東西南北每一個角落

信靠愛的滿全者　天主
在我們心中誕生
並永遠居住

# 尋

尋求真理
以祈禱
以詩
以你
以感謝

真理無所不在
唯可驗證的
你尋祂
祂尋你

# 南方之星

在我的窗口
遙望那一顆閃耀的南方之星

雖然都市的霓虹和燈火爭艷
在天際
那顆星還是最耀眼的挑動

思緒
在星子之上
你的眼睛

# 不管你怎麼說

我遇見一個獨行者
他說世界不缺誰
都照樣進行

的確
我們看見萬物
在每一個細節上
生動的進行
我們在意什麼　或
忽略什麼
世界都在鏗鏘前進

什麼事會讓我們停下腳步
或觸動堅硬的心
太陽不見一天
月亮不見一個月

誰在乎
詩又有何必要

差別在我堅信
堅信你和我同在

你引領我前進
沒有比這個更好的信念
使我做的事情更有意義
以你的眼光看世界
會超越我的眼界

我明白
愛是這樣流動
溫柔又堅定的充滿
世界因你而豐富多姿

# 嫉妒

嫉妒是一條無形的鋼索
絆倒自由
我們奉獻自己
任其捆綁
並甘願成為牠的奴隸

# 憂傷與快樂

憂傷
是釀不成酒
的醋
撥撥發酵
不知撩撥到
幾時

快樂
是葡萄美酒
香氣四溢
一不小心
就要
溢出一張小嘴

# 清晨的月亮

清晨的月亮
苦等不到一首詩

而繁華城市未眠的燈火
仍嘮嘮叨叨告解
深深淺淺的心事

黑眼圈的月亮
急著向黎明交稿

# 教會

教會仿若鏡子
亦是各色眼瞳掃視
站在前面的
照見係真實的自己

旅人書寫之詩篇
是腳前的驚嘆
不葷不素

# 基督之光

有一個人
住在荒山之巔
他不怕風聲像鬼慄哀號
他不怕黑夜緊緊籠罩
他仰望無盡的蒼天
讚歎主的奇妙創造

黑的層次
光的源頭
在浩瀚的宇宙
在自由的心靈
輕輕地
輕輕地拂過

光留在心裡
淚水滾燙周身
這一個人成為光

輕輕地
輕輕地走來

# 思念

在思念這個繩索上
輕輕握
一端　是
一端　不是

猜疑喜愛磨蹭著繩索
時間這個懶人
總是忘了時間

# 愛的故事萌芽的角落

心裡住著一個大人
心裡住著一個小人
心裡住著一個大小人
心裡住著一個小大人

心裡住下一個小小的人
足夠讓你有勇氣
足夠讓你的思想微笑

小小的角落
小小的
你在那裡

# 夢的途徑

香氛
也許是通往夢的途徑
撫慰遺失歲月的心靈

扮起調香師
一遍兩遍千遍
尋找你的氣息
深深呼吸

夢的氣息
混合著薰衣草與洋甘菊
還有玫瑰的苦澀

# 時空切片

汗水
淚水亦或
天降甘霖

時空切片

真理
隱藏在霧中

# 愛之頌

在無數個無數個原來如此
之後
我們仍然相信
愛是最大的慾望

儘管事實和時間對上了位置
快樂和痛苦各自找到出口

原來如此
原來是無懼的
兩個極端

認識彼此
我們的合唱
輝映最美麗的世界

# 鏡與湖

我靜默如一面鏡
美麗的人照見美麗
污穢的人照見污穢
純潔的人照見純潔
邪惡的人照見邪惡

我靜默如一面湖
小石仔也激起漣漪
一陣無心的風吹起浪花
留不住明月
收納你一串串的淚珠

# 真理的位置

被污水澆灌的田地
結出含毒素的果實
凡人的眼睛無法覺察
無言的肚腹卻一一收下

如果無言到底
這個世界終究是無言

智慧
在沒有道理的地方仍存在的力量
我們應束緊腰帶並緊緊跟隨

真理映現的
乃是我們走出的步步腳印

# 思月

如果月亮不見
月亮不見一天
你會知道嗎

如果月亮不見
夜空荒涼了兩天
你會憂傷嗎

每天見面的人
一天
兩天
三天
消失在你任何轉身之前

# 自由之鑰

天
沒有性別
主宰者
誰看見
大大大
大至你無法想的
小小小
小至你無法洞察
我的意念
和自己和天
和好

和好
乃握有自由之鑰

# 看天

相聚成一朵雲彩
在天際遨遊
想永遠是一朵雲彩般
自由
更自由的風
推擠
穿透
來自何方的風
來自海上
那亦屬於主所創造的
一切所創造的
無界

# 昨天

昨天
在心版上剛烙下印記的
熱
昨天的昨天
流落在無數星辰中的
一顆
心

# 想到你就高興

想到你就高興
這是我唯一可以不依靠你就可以做到的事

你的微笑
在每一個陌生人的臉上
你的純真
在每一個算計者的心中……
你的形影
在每一個孤單者的左右

想到你就深深呼吸
映現生命的芬芳氣息
選擇高興
這是我可以依靠自己就可以做到的事

# 樹蔭下的夢

如果
我的髮像濃密的樹葉
當風吹過
它會颼颼的響

我想
小雲雀一定喜歡
在樹上唱歌

當你微笑看著我
我會摘下一片無塵的夢想
送給你留作紀念

# 今朝茉莉

來不及看太陽下山
便紛紛離枝
潔白的
茉莉呀
在茶香裡漂浮

# 永恆的雕像

想擁有你
完美的形體
鋒芒
側身而過

刻畫你太難
保留亦或切割
日夜遲疑相繼

你是我將完成的雕像
彼此雕琢
不留自言自語

# 燭光

黑夜說
光　有什麼好？
把所有顏色聚在一起
醜陋　粗鄙都顯現出來

白晝說
黑　有什麼好？
把所有美善隱藏起來
看不見別人也看不清自己

蠟燭說
我願小小的光陪伴著你
不管白天黑夜
不管快樂或痛苦

# 擁抱

擁抱
開門第八件事

擁抱你的突刺
擁抱你的溫柔
擁抱你的快樂
擁抱你的沉默
擁抱你的原貌
擁抱你的氣息

每一天擁抱每一天
緊緊擁抱這個世界

# 生命之樹

生離死別
如落葉
層層覆蓋且撫育
生命之樹

生命之樹
堅挺啊
別怕長高　別怕孤單

最高的樹
將有星星作伴

# 愛的101

這個時代

充滿競賽

人們用房屋標誌著權力和慾望

高高的尖塔象徵著什麼

像一把利劍刺向天際的心臟

或像一把梯子藉它摘下最亮的星星

孩子純潔的心從小被訓練

學習累積高度

往更高的視野攀爬

然而

我們的心如何守候

適應這忽高忽低如坐雲霄飛車的環境

誰知道權力101的背後

誰知道財富101的背後

誰知道功名101的背後

誰知道美貌101的背後
所有成績所有成就101的背後

有沒有被冷落的101
有沒有黑暗的101
有沒有恐懼的101
有沒有醜陋的101
在失魂的陰暗角落哭泣

聖嬰的降臨
給人們啟示
另一個高度　愛的101
適合我們輕鬆的攀爬

愛的101
是我們的手牽著別人的手

愛的101
是別人的手牽著我們的手

心靈的夜空系列

# 信念

在所有的美好事物中看見你
或在所有醜陋中看見你的美好
這是堅硬的磐石

# 重要的想

重要和不重要在一樣的時間和不同的人會有不同反應如果
想了一天還想想下去而瞌睡蟲是不喜歡這個問題的輕重

# 門

一堆人在一起有時候也是雞同鴨講能夠說得上話又愉快的
真是讓人心情輕鬆愉快從早到晚我們走進走出什麼時候讓
我們感覺想留下甚至經裡說的搭帳篷留下或者想逃走為什
麼在人群中缺你會有很深的孤獨感

# 同一個月亮同一個音樂

聽同一個音樂在不同的地方也能找到相契合的地方心靈流動的地方自盤古開天自創世紀到現在的每一秒鐘音符就有這個承載能力看見最真實的世界這個世界最大的力量就來自這個起源超越所有藩籬是我的葡萄園有香松做的屋樑扁柏做的屋椽如茵的綠地而水仙和百合開放的多麼美麗

# 依靠

天氣很好其實就應該去散步去院子玩或聽你講話隨便亂講
都好可是總有很多不在我們前面就像以前看見跳箱就傻在
那裡不左一個右一個為什麼日子是這樣過在夢裡也會這樣
過嗎

# 心靈的夜空

只有在寂靜的夜空看得清楚自己和你和這個世界的有趣無趣和一些嘮嘮叨叨的人和有情無情卻也感覺美妙到甚至好玩好笑真是不知道怎麼會這麼高興所以就想亂寫一通考考你的眼睛怎麼讀這些字在夜空下天地都很大心靈的手腳也長長到就像可以拿下你的眼鏡今天寫這些避免你的眼睛痛今晚夜空漆黑沒法子在月亮裡看見你

# 土地和種子系列

1 在這個世界上不斷尋找圓滿，懷著信心尋找。

2 膽小鬼常常是自以為是的封閉。

3 你問我有什麼計畫？而，計畫總是那麼多，無從講起。
　只能馬上回答：一起吃早餐。

4 愛，偷工減料一定沒辦法完工。

5 靈修是尋覓可以打開心門的鑰匙。

6 說的時候要「問」，否則是白說。

7 願這個世界美麗不停。願自己成為可愛的人。

8 勇敢做自己，每一個生命都有不一樣的美麗。

9　在每一個地方都有一點「家」的味道。當我聽到這句話的時候心裡有說不出的孤寂感。「旅人」和「歸人」在行為上有不同定義。

10　愛　唯一的條件就是愛。

11　為什麼我喜歡樹，原來樹不會走。

12　我們的世界是一個「關係」的世界，我們建立的友好關係維繫著喜樂和生命力。是根和枝葉相連。

13 因為我相信你，所以跟隨你。〈最簡單的真理〉。

14 萬古長空，分秒必爭。爭著種瓜　種豆　種福！

15 方向清楚需要原則，後面有一個價值。

16 人生最珍貴的是愛和被愛。

17 好玩才會心情好，才有動力往前走。

18 人生當中讓我們學習最多的是：彼此的關係。

19 是事實不是爭辯。

20 痛苦不論是什麼痛苦，痛苦就是痛苦。不要讓我們依靠
自己，而要依靠天主。但是依靠天主是不自然的事，通
常我們都是依靠自己，靈修最難在此。

21 做「對」的事情，即使有阻力也要勇敢做下去。遇見
「對」的人，即使有破壞也要勇敢追隨。

22 法律能約束人的行為，而信仰能使人往上提升品格。

23 生命在自由中繁榮，宇宙有愛的秩序。

24 晴天也好雨天也好，白天也好黑夜也好，想也好不想也
好，雖然如此，並不表示我們是濫好人，而是，我們願
意做一個「好」的選擇。

25 在不妨害別人的自由和權利時，我們可以展現自己或取
　　所需，接納自己的真理。

26 每個人都有一個十字架；沒有任何一個十字架是羞恥
　　的。

27 在天主面前靜默，不要辯解。

28 留在天主的複雜度，不懂；但信任。

29 我們的時間就是播種子的時間。

30 天主的仁慈超過「人」的不義。

31 「微笑」是愛的禮物，輕巧又溫馨。

32 分心的人無法聽見你的聲音。

33 愛　是一個禮物；禮物打開來不能是空的。

34 恩寵等於驚喜，等於愛。

35 天主是喜樂的天主；祂不會創造一個亂七八糟的世界。

36 感恩是所有美善的開始。

37 花不言語，也傳遞生命的美麗。

38 天主要我們看清楚一切，但是要謙虛。

39 罪惡感是一個記號，太多的罪惡感會變成自卑感，影響
和天主的來往。

40 衣服用來遮蔽軟弱的地方。

41 不要勉強自己過不自然的生活。

42 不能把理想放在每一個人的身上，要尊重每一個人的不
一樣。

43 只有愛不受束縛。

44 生命的主角是我們自己。

45 信仰如果沒有喜樂，信仰和生活會格格不入。

46 一棵樹結出果實的好壞會讓我們知道這棵樹的好壞。

47 祈求寬恕比較容易寬恕。

48 只有愛可以解釋生命的痛苦和死亡。

49 自由的選擇也需要責任。

50 愛如果沒有行動，那也只是空談。

51 有權勢者控制這個世界改變這個世界，而愛是種子，小
小的種子一直存在。

52 生命的迷宮彎彎曲曲，要有在黑暗中行走的勇氣和容許
被引導的謙遜。

53 藝術容易和別人溝通，因為藝術是直接的，好就是好不用解釋。

54 害怕的時候，祈禱也不會輕鬆，克服害怕的第一步是醒過來，再來是祈禱。

55 回應恩寵，最美。

56 「白白給予愛你到底」當我們感受到這個精神，會讓我們脫離黑洞。

57 無條件的仁慈、無條件的愛、無條件的寬容。

58 不要給別人增加暴力的機會，保持立場就好。

59 沒有挑戰沒有成長；面對痛苦，愛的精神會出來。

60 天主要我們結出果實，不要我們停在好與不好的中間。

61 讓我們的每一個呼吸都成為聖神降臨的祈禱。

62 最好的時機就是「現在」。

63 淨化自己的記憶，以寬恕的態度待人，這樣我們的生活
　　會更好。

64 過去不會忘記，卻不是讓過去控制我們。

65 真善美是永恆的心靈地圖。

66 治癒來自親密，不是表演不是戴面具。

67 法律是內在的力量。

68 真理就是真理。不管我們用什麼角度去看。

69 自由是堅毅的翅膀，自由的翅膀能感受風的存在。

70 不要把注意力放在軟弱上。把注意力放在好的事情上，
軟弱的地方就會縮小。

71 團體中如果無法判斷是非就完了。需要判斷什麼是好是
壞？然後分辨清楚之後再包容。

72 可以選擇的時候都有自由。

73 我們的選擇會有一個結果，所以要先想好。

74 愛永遠在發芽，生生不息。

75 勇氣和慈愛放在一起，我就認出天主。

76 學習最好的工具就是生命。

77 生命中因「你」而變得勇敢，有價值。因「他」而豐富
　多變化。

78 你信的神是怎麼樣，你的態度就是怎麼樣。

79 當我們付出最好的一切，所有的付出都將成為豐富我們
　生活的養料。

80 人類真正的進步是將愛放入成就中。

81 相信許諾比掌握到許諾更重要。

# 作者簡介

　　鍾雲如，專長資源整合、大眾傳播。現任瑪利亞社會福利基金會董事，上慶傳播文化公司執行長。著有詩集《生命之樹》、《蒲公英的婚禮》、《時空切片》；繪本《不一樣的天使》；歌詞〈不一樣的天使〉、〈火中歸來〉、〈如果有愛〉、〈愛的米可〉等。

# 譯者簡介

孔維仁，義大利籍學者，及東方文化研究者。

# The South Star

# Mighty strength

What a mighty strength
Is hidden in the frailest of all lives,
In such tiny little lives

And feeble is their breath while crossing life's starting line,
Yet so powerful to awaken and summon this drowsy soul of mine,
Telling me softly:

"Love cannot wait".

# Rising above the bustling world

When you get too entangled with this bustling world,
Time dilutes into an indefinite infinite.
So, keep your focus! Not a moment to be wasted!

Do you want to grow melons?
Then praise melon growers.
Are you resolved to sow beans?
Then praise them, the beans sowers.

Ah! A genuine praise:
Could there be a more sweet-sounding melody than that?

# Quietly listen

(I want to quietly listen; yes, I'll be all ears … )

5 4 3 2 1  *(what are they saying? That's sheer absurdity!)*

1 2 3 4 5  *(oh, that's better, that makes more sense… )*

That is what I hear the wind whispering to me, only that.

How could I discern the truth inside that whisper?


Many harmonious sounds are filling this big world,

All kinds of melodies constantly resound in the air around us!

But sometimes, all of a sudden, here comes a discordant noise:

Then our hands instinctively go to cover our ears; we just refuse to listen!

Sure enough those piercing noises are about

5 4 3 2 1

1 2 3 4 5


Those noises say so much about how every person, each thing, every

     single sound

Are so powerfully alive,

And how we care about them all with intense emotions!

When a sense of hopelessness follows my sterile attempts to change,

Only God's voice is what I seek,

That He may guide me to rise above this cacophony of noises.

Oh, His voice, so sweet to my ears,

So full of peace.

# Seek

As a labyrinth which twists and turns, life,

As soon as we venture few steps into it,

Regularly intrigues and puzzles us;

And we, with dumb ears stiffed on our head,

Seem to aimlessly wander to and fro into the maze.


Search for truth,

Step by step, not in haste not too slow, gently,

Ready to seek it in every corner of the East and of the West,

Just for the sake of finding it.


Trust in Him, trust in Jesus:

Born in our hearts,

To dwell in them, forever.

# Quest

I am on a quest for truth:
Through prayer,
Through poetry,
Through you,
Through gratefulness.

Truth is omnipresent,
But how could you know it for sure? Only if
You look for Him,
He searches for you.

# The South Star

Gazing into the distance from my window,
I stare at the glittering South Star.

Neon lamps and other city lights are all vying for glamor,
But on the horizon, tonight, there is no match for this dazzling South Star:
It is the one capturing you with its breathtaking beauty.

And I can just feel,
In this little shining star,
Yes, your eyes.

# No Matter What You Say

I encountered a man, walking all alone.

He said, the world is good as it is, nothing wrong with it, no one is missing,

So, everything just goes on as usual.

Surely enough,

If we look at nature,

Every single detail

Is actively taken care of.

Whether we care so much for something or

We totally neglect something else,

The world will sonorously carry on as usual.

Something unexpected could slow down our steps

Or deeply touch our stony hearts;

The sun might disappear for one day,

So the moon for the whole month;

Yet, nobody would care;

And, by the way, are poems really necessary?

What really makes the difference is that I firmly believe,

Stubbornly believe, that you are here, together with me.

You lead me on my way ahead:

No belief is greater than this,

One which makes me do everything with a greater meaning!

To look at the world through your eyes

Makes me transcend my own worldview.

I finally realize

That this is exactly what the flow of love is:

A fullness which is warm, yet firm.

Because of you, the world is so abundantly rich in diversity!

# Jealousy

Jealousy is a steel cable with no shape nor core

You get entangled in it, and your freedom is gone.

Why should our self-giving

Become so binding, so restraining?

Why should our joyful willingness become jealousy's slave?

# Sorrow and Joy

Sorrow

Is like sour vinegar

——a wort which did not become wine

Constantly bubbling in its fermentation

I could not tell till when

Will it stir up?

Joy, on the other hand,

Is an excellent full bodied red wine

Suffusing an exquisite fragrance all around

It's easy, if you are not careful,

That it may spill

Over that little mouth!

# Morning moon

The morning moon hanging up just before dawn
Has a poem in its heart, but it doesn't come out! Oh, what an anguish!

Meanwhile, the lights of the bustling city that never sleeps,
Are still blabbering out stuff (sometimes deep, sometimes shallow),
As if making a long, interminable confession.

The moon has already dark circles under her eyes,
She is in a hurry to hand over the poem's draft to daybreak.

# The Church

The Church seems like a mirror
Or multi-colored pupils, standing right before you,
Constantly scanning all over the place;
What you will see reflected in them
Is just your true self.

The praising psalm written by the passing-by traveler
Is just an explosion of wonder at what he has briefly encountered;
What it describes is, nonetheless, neither fish nor fowl.

# The light of Christ

There is a man

Living on a barren mountain top.

He does not fear the wind screaming like a devil,

Nor the thick cover of the dark night.

He only fixes his eyes on the infinite vastness of the sky,

Gasping in admiration at the wonders of creation.


Different shades of darkness,

But with a source of light too,

In the vastness of the universe,

——As in a free spirit——

Both of them, darkness and light, softly,

Gently, pass by.


But that light remained in his heart,

While hot tears rolled down all over his body.

This man, he himself, became light

And softly,
Gently, He comes.

# Missing

I take into my hands the rope of nostalgia, that feeling of missing someone,

Holding gently

An extremity: oh, yes, that's it!

And the other end of the rope: oh no, it's not what I thought!

I'm getting suspicious at that dragging dawdling rope!

Time is truly a guy too lazy,

Always loosing track of itself…

# The corner sprouting love story

In the heart, there he lives——a Mr. Big.
In the heart, there he lives——a Mr. Small.
Sometimes Mr. Big is in charge,
Sometimes Mr. Small takes the chance.

In the heart there he lives,
A figure which towers no tall,
Yet sufficient for giving you courage,
And pleasuring your thoughts, hence.

In that small, small corner,
Small as it is,
You are there, as you are.

# The Doorway to Dreams

Perfume

Perhaps is simply a doorway leading to dreams,

The way to sooth the soul in anguish for the loss of the years gone-by.


Take on the perfumer's role,

Try again, once, twice, a thousand times,

To search for your scent,

Breathing in, breathing out——deeply.


The essence of my dream

Is a mélange of lavender and Chamomile

With a pungent bitter tinge of roses.

# A slice of time, a slice of space.

Is that sweat

Are they tears or

Simply Heaven-sent sweet refreshing drops of rain?


A slice of time, a slice of space.


Truth

Is somehow hidden in this moistened midst.

# Hymn To Love

"So, that was it ! Now I got it!"
Having said that again and again, for countless times,
We still, persistently believe that
Love is our greatest desire.

No matter how well reality and time have matched their positions,
Joy and pain have both found their way out and ahead!

"So, that was it! Now I got it!":
The desire of love and the apparent contradiction between joy and pain
Are actually two extreme feelings we need to fear not.

Our knowing each other,
And our singing together in one voice
Both brightly reflect what is most beautiful of our world.

# As A Mirror, As A Lake

I silently contemplate, as still as a mirror:

Beautiful people beam beauty;

Polluted people reflects pollution;

Pure people shine out purity

And it's only evil what evil people see.


I silently contemplate, as still as a lake,

Where a single peddle could stir long reaching ripples

And foaming waves can surge out of a single unwitting gust of wind;

Also, it cannot hold for long the bright moon:

Yet, it treasures each one of your tears as pearls in a necklace.

# Truth

Fields irrigated with polluted water

Have yielded toxic fruits;

An ordinary man's eyes cannot perceive it,

But his viscera will, silently, absorb those fruits,

One after the other.


If silent to the last,

This world will have nothing left to say.


Wisdom

Is like the bright mirror you are holding in your hand,

Is feeling the need to gird yourself

And get ready to follow, more closely.


And what truth is revealed, in the end,

Is only the footprints from the steps

Of our journey.

# Fondly missing the moon

If the moon would disappear,

Just disappear for one day,

Would you ever realize it?

If the moon would disappear,

Leaving a desolate sky for two days,

Would you have any sadness?

The people I use to meet every day,

After one day,

Two days,

Three days,

Oh, they can just disappear in front of you every time you turn 'round!

# The Key to Freedom

Heaven

Has not gender:

He, or She, rules it all.

But how does one knows it? Could anyone see the big, huge, vast,

So vast that you cannot imagine?

Or could anyone detail the tiny, little, small,

So small you can barely distinguish it?

Only when my thoughts

Are reconciled

Both with myself and with Heaven, then will I know it.


Only reconciliation

Holds the key to freedom.

# Gazing at the sky

Gathered together to form a huge pillar

Clouds are soaring upon the horizon.

Oh, I truly desire to be forever in that joyful gathering of clouds!

But here comes the wind, free,

the freest of all;

soon enough it pushes

and blows us apart.

Where does it come from, that wind?

From the four corners of the earth,

From the surface of the sea.

From all that belongs to God's creation,

And from every single creature:

Unbounded.

# Yesterday

Only yesterday

The wall of my heart was branded with a seal

Oh, branded with fire…

Could you believe it? Just the day before yesterday

That same, same heart

Was up there, all alone,

Stranded

Amongst millions of constellations…

# Whenever I think of you, I feel so joyful!

Whenever I think of you, I feel so joyful!
This may be the only thing I can do without relying on you.

Your smile
Shines on the face of every stranger;
Your innocence
Dwells in the heart of those who are always plotting something;
Your shadow
Is companion to everyone who feels lonely.

Whenever I think of you, I will take a deep breath, in and out,
Effusing around the sweet scent of life-breath.
The choice to be joyful
Is the only thing I can do just relying on myself.

# A dream under the shade of a tree

If my hair
Were like the dense foliage of this tree,
Then the wind would blow into them
With a whooshing sound.

I think that
In that moment the skylark would surely enjoy
To sing on that tree!

When you are looking at me, smiling,
I wish I could pick down an uncontaminated pure dream
And give it to you, for you to remember.

# Today's Jasmine Flowers

They could not wait for the setting of the sun:

Instead, one after the other, falling from their branches,

The pure white

Jasmine flowers

Were like floating in the warm aroma of tea.

# Timeless Statue

I wish I could possess you,

Perfect figure!

But my chisel

Simply passes you by like a caress.


It would be too difficult to portray you

What to retain? What to cut out?

I always think of it, as if day and night hesitate to take over from each other.


You are the statue I will one day complete:

We will carve each other

And not anymore withhold any word

We previously only murmured within ourselves.

# Candlelight

The night said
"Light, don't brag about yourself! What good do you have?
You just mix together all the colors
And clearly exposed both the ugly and the vulgar ".

The daylight replied:
"Darkness, don't brag about yourself, what good do you have?"
You hide in yourself all what is beautiful and good,
You don't clearly see neither yourself nor the others.

So said the candle:
"I am available to offer my small little light to be your companion,
Be it in daylight or in the dark night
Be it in joy or in pain"

# Embrace

An embrace:

There is need to add that as "The Eighth Necessity" to start the day with.

Embrace your protruding thorns,

And embrace your warmth too;

Embrace your joy,

Embrace your silence...

Embrace your original "you",

And embrace your breath as well.

Everyday embrace the new day

And hug tightly this big, big world.

# The Tree of Life

Separations in life and farewells at death,
Like falling leaves,
Layer by layer cover and nurture
The Tree of Life.

Oh, Tree of life,
Keep standing, firm and upright!
Don't be afraid of growing tall, nor fear loneliness!

The highest trees
Will have stars as companions.

# Love's 101

Competition

Permeates our times.

We even use buildings to express power and ambition.

What does this steep tower symbolize anyway?

A sharp dagger piercing the heart of the horizon

Or a ladder for harvesting the most shining stars in the sky?


Since infancy, children's pure hearts are trained

To learn how to reach new height,

How to scramble for places with better perspectives.

And at the same time

How to prevent our hearts from being harmed

By the ups and downs of the endless roller coaster on which we
spend our lives?


Does anybody know what's behind the power of 101,

And the wealth of 101,

And the fame of 101,

And the charm of 101,

Does anybody know if behind all the successes and achievements of 101?


Is there a 101 which is desolate?

Or a 101 lost in darkness?

Is there a 101 paralyzed by fear?

Or a 101 which feels its own ugliness,

Weeping soullessly in a dark corner?


The descent of the Holy Infant,

Opens humanity to the revelation

About another summit——Love's 101:

The only one reachable by our unencumbered ascent.


Love's 101

Is our hands holding others'.

Love's 101

Is other's hands holding ours!

# About the Author

Chung Yun-ru has been engaging in mass media and social welfare work quite a long time. Currently, she is a director of Maria Social Welfare Foundation, and CEO of SCBC Dissemination of Culture, Ltd. Her collections of poetry include *"The Tree of Life" Life"*, *"The Wedding of Dandelion"*, *"Time after taking Food and Drinks "*, *"Seven Strings "* and *"No Reason is needed for Writing Poems"*, as well as a children book *"Not the Same Angel"*.

# About the Translator

Consonni Paolo, Italian scholar and researcher of Asian cultures.

# CONTENTS

語言文學類　PG1757　台灣詩叢03

# 南方之星 The South Star
## ──鍾雲如漢英雙語詩集

作　　者 / 鍾雲如（Chung Yun-ru）
譯　　者 / 孔維仁（Consonni Paolo）
叢書策劃 / 李魁賢（Lee Kuei-shien）
責任編輯 / 林昕平
圖文排版 / 周妤靜
封面設計 / 葉力安

發 行 人 / 宋政坤
法律顧問 / 毛國樑　律師
出版發行 / 秀威資訊科技股份有限公司
　　　　　114台北市內湖區瑞光路76巷65號1樓
　　　　　電話：+886-2-2796-3638　傳真：+886-2-2796-1377
　　　　　http://www.showwe.com.tw
劃撥帳號 / 19563868　戶名：秀威資訊科技股份有限公司
　　　　　讀者服務信箱：service@showwe.com.tw
展售門市 / 國家書店（松江門市）
　　　　　104台北市中山區松江路209號1樓
　　　　　電話：+886-2-2518-0207　傳真：+886-2-2518-0778
網路訂購 / 秀威網路書店：http://www.bodbooks.com.tw
　　　　　國家網路書店：http://www.govbooks.com.tw

2017年5月　BOD一版
定價：200元
版權所有　翻印必究
本書如有缺頁、破損或裝訂錯誤，請寄回更換

國家圖書館出版品預行編目

南方之星 The South Star: 鍾雲如漢英雙語詩集 /
鍾雲如著 ; 孔維仁譯. -- 一版. -- 臺北市 : 秀
威資訊科技, 2017.05
　　面 ；　公分. -- (語言文學類)(臺灣詩叢 ; 3)
BOD版
ISBN 978-986-326-418-7(平裝)

851.486　　　　　　　　　　　106003912

# 讀者回函卡

感謝您購買本書,為提升服務品質,請填妥以下資料,將讀者回函卡直接寄
回或傳真本公司,收到您的寶貴意見後,我們會收藏記錄及檢討,謝謝!
如您需要了解本公司最新出版書目、購書優惠或企劃活動,歡迎您上網查詢
或下載相關資料: http:// www.showwe.com.tw

您購買的書名:＿＿＿＿＿＿＿＿＿＿＿＿＿＿＿＿＿＿＿＿＿＿

出生日期:＿＿＿＿＿年＿＿＿＿＿月＿＿＿＿日

學歷:□高中 (含) 以下　　□大專　　□研究所 (含) 以上

職業:□製造業　□金融業　□資訊業　□軍警　□傳播業　□自由業
　　　□服務業　□公務員　□教職　　□學生　□家管　　□其它＿＿＿＿

購書地點:□網路書店　□實體書店　□書展　□郵購　□贈閱　□其他

您從何得知本書的消息?

　□網路書店　□實體書店　□網路搜尋　□電子報　□書訊　□雜誌
　□傳播媒體　□親友推薦　□網站推薦　□部落格　□其他＿＿＿＿＿＿

您對本書的評價:(請填代號　1.非常滿意　2.滿意　3.尚可　4.再改進)

　封面設計＿＿＿　版面編排＿＿＿　內容＿＿＿　文／譯筆＿＿＿　價格＿＿＿

讀完書後您覺得:

　□很有收穫　□有收穫　□收穫不多　□沒收穫


對我們的建議:＿＿＿＿＿＿＿＿＿＿＿＿＿＿＿＿＿＿＿＿＿＿＿

＿＿＿＿＿＿＿＿＿＿＿＿＿＿＿＿＿＿＿＿＿＿＿＿＿＿＿＿＿＿＿

＿＿＿＿＿＿＿＿＿＿＿＿＿＿＿＿＿＿＿＿＿＿＿＿＿＿＿＿＿＿＿

＿＿＿＿＿＿＿＿＿＿＿＿＿＿＿＿＿＿＿＿＿＿＿＿＿＿＿＿＿＿＿

11466
台北市內湖區瑞光路 76 巷 65 號 1 樓

**秀威資訊科技股份有限公司**　　　收

BOD 數位出版事業部

⋯⋯⋯⋯⋯⋯⋯⋯⋯⋯⋯⋯⋯⋯⋯⋯⋯⋯⋯⋯⋯⋯⋯⋯

（請沿線對折寄回，謝謝！）


姓　　名：＿＿＿＿＿＿＿＿　年齡：＿＿＿＿　性別：□女　□男

郵遞區號：□□□□□

地　　址：＿＿＿＿＿＿＿＿＿＿＿＿＿＿＿＿＿＿＿＿＿

聯絡電話：(日) ＿＿＿＿＿＿＿＿＿　(夜) ＿＿＿＿＿＿＿＿＿

E-mail：＿＿＿＿＿＿＿＿＿＿＿＿＿＿＿＿＿＿＿＿＿